How D Take Baths?

By Diane Muldrow
Illustrated by David Walker

A GOLDEN BOOK • NEW YORK

rhcbooks.com
Educators and librarians, for a variety of teaching tools, visit us at RHTeachersLibrarians.com
Library of Congress Control Number: 2020930120
ISBN 978-0-593-12777-3 (trade) — ISBN 978-0-593-12778-0 (ebook)
Printed in the United States of America
10 9 8 7 6 5 4 3 2 1

Cats lick their fur
to keep it soft and neat.

Gorillas pick off ticks,
from their faces to their feet.

Bobcats . . .

and giraffes
clean their ears each day.

Bunnies lick their ears *a-a-a-l-l-l* the way!

Chickens shake off bugs
in the cool, dry dust.

So do quail and bison, when they must.

Tiny ticks can be good to munch.
This zebra's pest is
the oxpecker's lunch!

Owls keep clean with the heat from the sun.

This elephant's bath
looks like lots of fun!

Barbel fish are a hippo's best friend—
they nibble off gunk from end to end!

Dogs shake, scratch, and bite
each pesky flea and tiny dust mite.

Tigers love to soak
in a cold lake or stream.

Macaques relax in hot-water steam!

Beavers comb their fur
to remove what's cruddy.

Rhinos roll around
in a bath
that's muddy!

Sparrows splish-splash,
and then they preen
until they are bug-free,
cool, and clean!

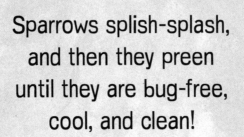